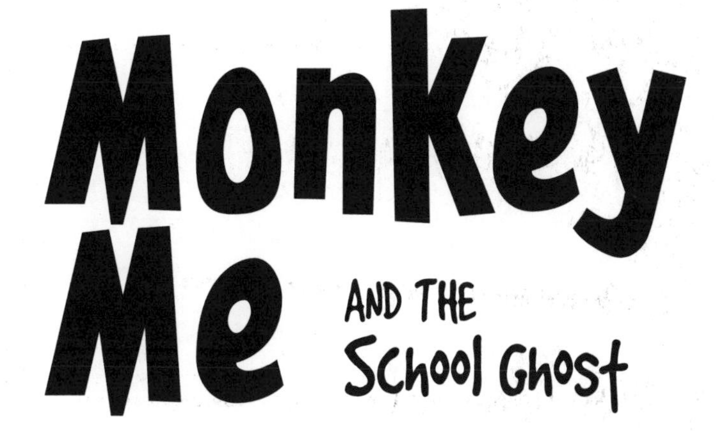

Monkey Me AND THE School Ghost

BY
TIMOTHY ROLAND

SCHOLASTIC INC.

Read all the **Monkey Me** books!

Table of Contents

Thanks Matt Ringler (editing) and Liz Herzog (design) for your help in getting an out-of-control monkey (and boy) into these books.
-T.R.

Library of Congress Cataloging-in-Publication-Data Available

ISBN 978-0-545-55990-4 (hardcover)/ ISBN 978-0-545-55989-8 (paperback)

10 9 8 7 6 5 4 3 2 1 14 15 16 17 18 19/0

Printed in China 38
First Scholastic printing, October 2014
Book design by Liz Herzog

Chapter 1
Monkey News

"Calm down, Clyde!" Claudia, my twin sister, said.

"Ha! See you later, alligator!" I said.

I raced up the steps and into the science museum. "Yippee!" I slid across the floor of the main lobby.

"Slow down!" a museum guard yelled.

I kept sliding. Then I ran.

There was lots I wanted to see!

Dinosaurs! Mummies! The Golden Monkey! The stuffed gorilla!

"Clyde!" Claudia held onto my shoulder. "We're not here to see the exhibits!" she said. "We're here to see Dr. Wally."

"Rats!" I said.

My sister pulled me toward a back room in the museum. It is where Dr. Wally does his science experiments.

It was where I became the monkey me.

IT HAPPENED THREE WEEKS AGO AT THE MUSEUM. I WAS HUNGRY.
SO I ATE A BANANA THAT WAS PART OF AN EXPERIMENT.
DR. WALLY TOLD ME IT CHANGED THE WAY MY BODY WORKS.
NOW, WHEN I GET SUPER EXCITED...
I CHANGE INTO A **MONKEY**!

"This way, Clyde!" Claudia held my arm tightly. She pulled me into a back room at the museum.

"Welcome, Clyde and Claudia," Dr. Wally said. "How may I help you?"

"We were hoping you found a cure," Claudia said. "Something that will stop Clyde from changing into a monkey."

"I'm working on it," Dr. Wally said. "And I need to find the cure quickly."

He looked at me closely.

I looked at the open doorway. I couldn't wait to leave and see the museum exhibits outside the back room.

"The more Clyde changes into a monkey," Dr. Wally said, "the more chance there is of him not being able to change back into a boy."

Claudia gasped.

I walked toward the doorway.

"You mean, my brother could be a real monkey forever?" Claudia asked.

Dr. Wally nodded.

"Did you hear that, Clyde?" Claudia asked.

I did. Sort of. I was halfway across the room. And I was super excited. And I was bouncing. Higher. And higher.

"Clyde! Stop!" Claudia yelled.

"I can't." I bounced into the hallway.

Then my head started spinning. My heart raced. Faster. And faster.

I sneezed.

Chapter 2
Museum Monkey

COME BACK, CLYDE!
HERE I GO AGAIN.

TA-DAH!
ARE YOU CRAZY, CLYDE?! YOU MIGHT STAY A MONKEY FOREVER!
AND YOU MIGHT GET IN TROUBLE! AND . . .
CLYDE?!
TIME TO HAVE FUN!

CLYDE GOT AWAY, DR. WALLY.
WE'LL SPLIT UP AND FIND HIM.
WHERE COULD THE MONKEY BE?
THERE HE IS!
HA-HA!
AND THERE HE GOES.
HA-HA!

THE MONKEY HAS TO BE HERE.
BUT WHERE?
I'LL LOOK THIS WAY.
I'LL LOOK THIS WAY.

WOW! THE GOLDEN MONKEY!
AND THE STUFFED GORILLA!
SOMEONE'S COMING! I SHOULD HIDE!
THE MONKEY HAS TO BE HERE SOMEWHERE!
BUT WHERE?

THIS MUSEUM HAS SO MANY FUN THINGS TO SEE.
WHY WOULD I EVER WANT TO LEAVE?
CLYDE! IF WE DON'T LEAVE SOON...
...WE MIGHT MISS SUPPER!
SUPPER?!
HERE'S YOUR CLOTHES, CLYDE.
YIPPEE!

OF COURSE, BEFORE WE CAN EAT...
...WE'LL NEED TO DO OUR HOMEWORK.
HOMEWORK?!

Chapter 3
Monkey-in-the-Middle

"Are you okay, Clyde?" Claudia asked.

I paused. I looked.

I was human again!

"See," I said to Claudia. "I didn't change into a monkey forever."

I quickly dressed. Then I raced out of the museum and down the front steps.

Claudia ran after me. "Next time you change, Clyde," she said, "you might not be able to change back into a boy."

"So?" I said.

"You would be a monkey. Forever!" Claudia said.

I grinned."That might be fun."

"Not for me," Claudia said. "I don't want to lose you as my brother."

I looked at my sister's worried face. I didn't know what to say. So I hopped on my bike and pedaled toward home.

Claudia followed.

When I got home, I quickly finished my homework. Well, almost.

Then I ate supper. YUM!

After supper, Mom held up two large paper bags.

"Claudia. Clyde," Mom said. "These are the costumes I bought you for tomorrow's Halloween party."

Mom handed Claudia a bag.

"Yippee!" Claudia yelled when she opened it. "I'm going to be an astronaut!"

My sister hopes to one day become a real astronaut and fly in a rocket to the moon.

Mom handed me the other bag.

"Well, Clyde," Claudia asked, "what are you going to be?"

I held up my costume. "I'm going to be . . . a MONKEY!" I shouted.

Claudia gasped.

Mom smiled. "I bought it for you, Clyde," she said, "because I know how much you like monkeys."

"Thanks, Mom!" I ran to my bedroom to try on my costume!

Claudia quickly followed. She held on to one arm of my monkey costume.

"Wearing this at the Halloween party will get you too excited, Clyde" Claudia said.

"But it's my costume!" I said.

"Not anymore!" Claudia pulled it from me. "Here!" She handed me her astronaut costume. "We're switching."

I looked at my new costume.

Okay, being an astronaut was not going to be as much fun as being a monkey.

But I was still really excited.

Chapter 4

Scary, Scary Roz

The next morning I ran out of my house and toward school.

"Come back!" Claudia yelled.

Ha! I was excited about the Halloween party. Nothing could make me go back.

"You forgot your costume!" Claudia said.

Oops! Except that.

I raced back to my house.

Claudia handed me my backpack. It was full and heavy. Inside was my costume.

"If I put the astronaut costume on," I said, "maybe I could fly. Then I could get to school super fast!"

"Stop being silly, Clyde!" Claudia said. "And don't even think about costumes until it's time for the party."

I followed as my sister walked toward school. Her backpack was full, like mine. And I knew what was inside.

I pictured Claudia in the monkey costume and laughed. Then I ran onto the school playground and —

KA-BAM!

Suddenly, I was on the ground.

"Ha-ha! Squashed you!" Roz said.

I stared up at the class bully. She looked scary — even without a Halloween mask on.

My sister stepped in front of Roz and glared. "Leave Clyde alone!" Claudia said.

"Make me!" Roz glared at Claudia.

My sister is smart. She is good at getting me out of trouble with Roz. But this time, Claudia ran away.

"Chicken!" Roz laughed at Claudia. Then she looked at me. "Now run, little bug!"

I wobbled to my feet.

Roz gave me a shove. "Run!" she said.

I did.

I am usually faster than Roz. But my backpack was full. I heard footsteps behind me getting closer. And closer. Then —

I was on the ground.

"Ha-ha! Squashed you again, little bug!" Roz said.

I looked up at Roz. But I didn't move. I hoped the bully would go away.

Just then Claudia stepped in front of Roz. "Leave my brother alone!" my sister yelled.

"Look!" Roz said. "The chicken's back."

"And I brought help," Claudia said.

"Ha! Whoever you brought, I'll squash them, too!" Roz said.

Claudia grinned.

"So, who did you bring?" Roz asked.

Someone behind Roz tapped her on the shoulder.

Roz spun around. Her eyes opened super wide when she saw Principal Murphy.

Our principal glared. Then she led Roz across the playground and toward the office.

I looked at Claudia and smiled. My sister is smart. And Roz was gone.

At least, for a while.

Chapter 5
Halloween Fun

The bell rang and I dashed into the school building.

"Slow down!" a tall woman I had never seen before yelled. She was standing in the hallway holding a mop.

She looked angry. I think. I raced past her too fast to really see.

I ran into my classroom.

"Slow down, Clyde!" Miss Plum, my teacher, jumped up from her desk.

"I can't," I said. "I'm too excited."

"Clyde!" Miss Plum yelled.

My body stopped. But my mind kept racing.

"When can I put on my costume?" I asked. I pulled off my backpack.

Miss Plum stopped me from opening it.

"The Halloween party isn't until this afternoon, Clyde," she said.

"I can't wait!" I said as I bounced.

"I think you need a job, Clyde," Miss Plum said as I bounced higher.

She handed me some paper Halloween decorations to tape up around the room.

Miss Plum often gives me jobs to do in the classroom. She says it is a good way for me to use up some of my extra energy.

But after I finished decorating, I still had lots of energy left.

I sat at my desk and bounced.

I was excited about the Halloween party.

I was also excited because Roz was still in the office.

"Calm down, Clyde," Claudia said. My sister sits at the desk next to mine. "Or you could turn into a monkey! Forever!"

"I'll try," I said. But next we made paper pumpkins in art class.

And I couldn't slow down. Or keep paste off my desk. Or my shirt.

"What is that supposed to be?" Claudia asked when I held up my finished project.

"It's a pumpkin monkey," I said.

I laughed and laughed. Until after lunch, when Roz returned.

Principal Murphy also walked into my classroom. She was carrying a purse. She set it next to Miss Plum's desk.

The principal opened the purse, pulled out a paper crown, and stuck it on her head.

It was her costume. I think.

"Principal Murphy is here to see you in your costumes, class," Miss Plum said. "So it's time to change."

"Yippee!" I raced to the boys' bathroom. "It's party time!"

Chapter 6
Costumes

I changed into my astronaut costume. I tried to fly but couldn't. So I ran back to class.

I dashed past what looked like a large butterfly. Or a large fairy. Or —

"Calm down, Clyde!" Miss Plum said as she finished putting on her wings.

I looked at the paper bats, ghosts, and Halloween pumpkins on the walls.

I hurried to the food table. I saw apples. And muffins. And jellybeans! YUM!

I spun around as kids in their costumes danced into the classroom.

A pirate. A clown. A princess. A ghost who walked over and knocked me down.

"Roz?" I said.

The bully ghost laughed and walked away.

I stood and looked around. The Halloween party was about to begin!

I bounced.

Someone grabbed my arm. "Calm down, Clyde!" she said.

I turned and saw my sister wearing her monkey costume.

I couldn't stop laughing. Or bouncing.

"You're getting too excited!" Claudia said. She pulled me into the hallway.

My head started spinning.

My heart raced. Faster. And faster.

I sneezed. "A-CHOO!"

TA-DAH!
CLYDE?!
CLAUDIA?!
THIS IS ALMOST LIKE LOOKING IN A MIRROR.
YOU NEED TO GET BACK TO CLASS, CLYDE!
THAT'S WHERE I'M GOING, CLAUDIA.

BUT FIRST, YOU NEED TO CHANGE BACK INTO A BOY!
HA! IT'S PARTY TIME!
I CAN'T WAIT!
I CAN'T WATCH.
WOW! GREAT PARTY!
GREAT CROWN!

BUMP!
UH-OH! ROZ!
TIME TO PLAY!

UH-OH!
UH-OH!
CRASH!
OOPS!

TIME TO LEAVE.
HOW WAS THE PARTY, CLYDE?
MESSY.

I COULD USE MY MONKEY SPEED...
... AND TRY TO OUTRUN THEM.
OR I COULD USE MY MONKEY BRAIN...
... AND HIDE!

THERE GOES PRINCIPAL MURPHY.
THERE GOES ROZ.
THERE GOES...
WAIT! THAT SECOND GHOST ISN'T ROZ!
THAT GHOST IS TALL, WEARING WORK BOOTS, AND CARRYING A PURSE!

GET BACK TO YOUR CLASSROOM, ROZ!
HA! SHE DOESN'T KNOW WHO I AM!
AND SHE'S TOO BUSY TO STOP ME AND FIND OUT!
I NEED TO CATCH THAT MONKEY!
GOOD! I LOST PRINCIPAL MURPHY!

CLYDE?! ARE YOU OKAY?
I SAW A GHOST, CLAUDIA.
YOU SAW ROZ?
YES. BUT I ALSO SAW A TALL GHOST WITH A PURSE!
ARE YOU SURE YOU'RE OKAY?
NO. I'M...
I'M...
HUMAN AGAIN.
HERE'S YOUR COSTUME.
NOW LET'S GET BACK TO CLASS.

"You're in super big trouble this time, Clyde!" Claudia ran in front of me toward our classroom.

"No, I'm not," I said. "Everyone saw a monkey mess up the classroom, not me."

And I was right. When we stepped into the room, a net swung down — on top of Claudia!

"Ha-ha!" Principal Murphy shouted. She had gotten her big net from the office. "I caught the monkey!"

Miss Plum looked at what was under the principal's net. "Or someone wearing a monkey costume," my teacher said

Principal Murphy carefully lifted the net.

My sister stood perfectly still.

Like a monkey statue.

Everyone stared.

"Take off your mask!" Principal Murphy ordered.

At first, Claudia didn't move. Or speak. Then, she pulled off her monkey mask.

"Claudia?" Principal Murphy said. "I can't believe it was a nice girl like you who messed up the classroom."

"I believe it!" someone behind me said.

I turned and saw a ghost. But I knew it was Roz in her costume.

"Claudia is a troublemaker," Roz said. "Just like her brother, Clyde."

"But I didn't mess up our classroom!" Claudia said.

"We saw you," Principal Murphy said.

"No, you didn't," I said.

Everyone stared at me.

Claudia was always helping me get out of trouble. Now it was my turn to help her.

"Claudia can't climb a wall . . . or swing by her tail," I said. "Only a real monkey can do that."

Principal Murphy scratched her head.

"There were two monkeys," I said. "A real one, and Claudia in her costume."

"And it was the real monkey who messed up the classroom?" Principal Murphy asked.

I nodded.

"And it was the real monkey who got away from me again!" Principal Murphy said.

I nodded and grinned.

Principal Murphy looked angry as she walked to Miss Plum's desk. Then she looked even angrier.

"My purse is missing!" she screamed.

Principal Murphy looked on the other side of the teacher's desk. She looked under the desk. "Who took my purse?" she asked.

She looked around the messy classroom.

"Wait a minute!" Principal Murphy said. "That was my purse I saw in the hallway. And it was a ghost who took it. Or someone dressed like a ghost!"

Everyone stared at Roz, who was wearing a ghost costume.

"Come with me, Roz!" Principal Murphy took her to the office.

Chapter 8
The Truth

The tall woman wearing work boots that I had seen earlier stepped into the classroom.

"Her name is Miss Mopper," Miss Plum told the class. "She is the substitute janitor for this week."

Miss Mopper's face turned red and angry as she stared at the messy room.

"Party's over!" Miss Mopper yelled.

She made the class stay after school and clean the room. When we had finished, my sister and I headed home.

"You need to stop changing into a monkey, Clyde," Claudia said. "Because when you do, you usually get in trouble."

My sister grabbed my arm. "Or you get *me* in trouble!"

"But I got you out of trouble, too," I said.

Claudia let go of my arm.

We walked home and upstairs.

"Can you believe that Roz stole Principal Murphy's purse today?" Claudia asked.

"Not really." I walked down the hallway.

"Stealing is super bad," Claudia said. She followed me into my bedroom. "Roz will probably be taken out of our school."

"Really?" I asked.

Claudia nodded. "The bully will be out of your life. Forever!"

I took off my backpack. I dropped it on the floor.

"Just think, Clyde," Claudia said. "No more being knocked down. Or being chased by Roz around the playground."

I sat on the edge of my bed and frowned.

"I thought you'd be happy," Claudia said.

"I am," I said. Or at least, I should have been. But my stomach felt a little sick.

Claudia looked at me closely. As twins, we sometimes knew what the other was thinking or feeling.

"What's wrong, Clyde?" Claudia asked.

"I saw two ghosts in the hallway," I said. "It was the tall ghost, not Roz, who stole the purse."

"But Principal Murphy thinks Roz is the thief," Claudia said.

"I know," I said.

"So Roz is going to get punished for something she didn't do," Claudia said.

I tried to smile, but I couldn't.

"You are the only person who can get Roz out of trouble, Clyde," Claudia said.

"I know," I said. "But Roz has never been nice to me. So why should I help her?"

Claudia didn't answer. She didn't have to.

I knew that telling Principal Murphy the truth was the right thing to do. Even if it meant Roz would stay in my school.

"Okay. I'll tell the principal tomorrow," I said softly.

Claudia grinned.

I grinned, too.

Chapter 9
A Monkey Forever?

Eating supper made my stomach feel much better. We had meatloaf. And mashed potatoes. And corn.

And for dessert, we had banana pudding!

YUM! It was my favorite!

I ate two big bowls of banana pudding. Then I raced upstairs to my bedroom.

I felt super!

I bounced on my bed.

"Calm down, Clyde!" Claudia said as she rushed into my bedroom. "If you're not careful, you'll turn into a —"

"A monkey!" I laughed.

I bounced higher.

Then my head started spinning. My heart raced. Faster. And faster.

I sneezed. "A-CHOO!"

TA-DAH!
OH, NO! THE MONKEY!
WHERE?
CLYDE! STOP MONKEYING AROUND!
WHY?
YOU MIGHT GET IN TROUBLE.
YOU MIGHT NOT BE ABLE TO TURN BACK INTO A BOY.
SO?

YOU CAN'T BE A MONKEY FOREVER!
WHY NOT? SOUNDS LIKE FUN.
YOU'LL MISS BEING A BOY...
...AND BEING MY BROTHER.
YOU'LL SEE, CLYDE!
I HOPE.

I CAN LIVE WITH MY FRIEND AND NEIGHBOR, MUFFIN.
OKAY, SO SHE'S PRINCIPAL MURPHY'S CAT.
BUT MUFFIN KNOWS HOW TO HAVE FUN.
WHEN SHE'S NOT TAKING A NAP.
WHICH SHE DOES A LOT.

BEING A MONKEY FOREVER WILL BE LOTS OF FUN.
I HAVE EVERYTHING I NEED.
EXCEPT A BED TO SLEEP IN.
AND A GOOD MEAL TO EAT.
AND A FUNNY BOOK TO READ.

YOU'RE A GOOD FRIEND, MUFFIN.
BUT I NEED SOMEONE TO TALK TO...
...WHO TALKS BACK.
LIKE MOM.
AND DAD.
AND...
CLAUDIA!
CLYDE!

OKAY. SO I CAN'T BE A MONKEY FOREVER.
BUT CAN YOU CHANGE BACK INTO A BOY?
NO PROBLEM. I JUST NEED TO THINK OF SOMETHING SAD.
LIKE THIS.
SEE.
YOU DIDN'T CHANGE, CLYDE!
UH-OH!

I CAN'T CHANGE BACK.
WHICH MAKES ME SUPER WORRIED.
AND...
IT'S HAPPENING!
CLYDE?!

Chapter 10
Monkey Ears

I stood and looked at my body. "See, Claudia," I said. "There was nothing to worry about. I changed back."

Claudia's eyes opened super wide as she stared at me.

"What's wrong?" I asked.

She pointed at my face.

"Your ears!" Claudia shouted.

"What about them?" I asked.

"Look in the mirror, Clyde!" Claudia said.

I ran to my bedroom mirror. I looked at my face. And at my super-large ears!

"Yikes!" I said.

I looked in the mirror again.

"I have monkey ears!" I shouted. "But why? What happened?"

"You didn't change all the way back into a boy," Claudia said. She stared at my ears.

"I can't believe this!" I said. "What will Mom and Dad say? And the kids at school?"

I pulled hard on my super-large ears.

"Ouch!" I yelled.

The monkey ears were stuck to the sides of my human face. "How do I get rid of them?" I asked.

"I know who might know," Claudia said. She grabbed a phone and called the science museum. She told Dr. Wally that I now had monkey ears.

"What should Clyde do, Dr. Wally?" Claudia asked.

She listened for a moment. Then she thanked Dr. Wally and hung up the phone.

"What did he say?" I asked my sister.

"He said that until he finds a cure that stops you from turning into a monkey," Claudia replied, "there's nothing he can do to help."

"So what should I do until he finds a cure?" I asked. I looked again in the mirror.

"Dr. Wally said you need to stop getting excited," Claudia said.

"I know that!" I yelled. I pointed to my monkey ears. "What did Dr. Wally say I should do about these?"

Claudia ran to my closet. She picked up something and turned to face me.

"Here, Clyde!" Claudia tossed me a winter hat. "Wear this!"

I put on the hat. I stretched it down on the sides so it covered my monkey ears.

Then I looked in my mirror.

I looked silly with the hat on. But, with my big monkey ears, I looked even sillier with the hat off.

Chapter 11
Secrets

The next morning I put on my hat.

"How will you get past Mom and Dad without them asking any questions, Clyde?" Claudia asked.

"Like this," I said. I ran downstairs and grabbed a banana off the breakfast table. Then I raced out the front door.

Claudia ran after me. "It worked," she said when she caught up.

I grinned. Then I dashed to school and onto the playground.

Some kids said, "Nice hat, Clyde." But most didn't seem to notice. Or care.

Of course, Roz would have noticed.

She would have knocked me down and taken my hat.

Then, when she would have seen my monkey ears, she would have laughed. And laughed. And laughed.

I'm glad Roz wasn't around.

But I still had to tell Principal Murphy the truth: Roz wasn't the purse thief.

"I'll tell her at the end of the day," I said to myself as I walked to my classroom.

Miss Plum was happy to see I was walking, not running. But she asked why I was wearing the hat.

I didn't know what to say.

But Claudia did. "Wearing the hat keeps Clyde from getting too excited and causing trouble," she told Miss Plum.

Miss Plum grinned a little. Then she said I could keep the hat on . . . as long as I stayed calm and behaved.

I said I would.

I didn't want anyone to see my monkey ears. And I hoped if I stayed calm, they would shrink back to human size.

But at the end of the school day, my ears were still super large. So I wore my hat as I walked with Claudia to the principal's office.

Principal Murphy was sitting at her big desk. Next to the desk was her new purse.

I told Principal Murphy that Roz didn't steal her other purse.

"But I saw her with the purse," Principal Murphy said.

"No, you didn't," I said. "You saw a ghost with your purse."

"And Roz was dressed in a ghost costume!" Principal Murphy said.

"There were two ghosts in the hallway yesterday," I said. "It was the tall ghost, not Roz, who stole your purse."

"How do you know, Clyde?" Principal Murphy asked.

"I saw the whole thing," I said.

The principal looked at me like she thought I was making up a story.

I knew she probably wouldn't believe me, unless someone caught the ghost thief.

"But it really is true!" I said. "Roz didn't take your purse!"

Principal Murphy leaned across her desk. She looked at me closely. Then she told me to take off my hat.

Chapter 12
It's Monkey Time!

"Take off your hat please, Clyde!" Principal Murphy said again.

I gulped. If I took off my hat, she would see my monkey ears. And then —

The office door burst open. "The monkey is in the hallway!" Miss Mopper yelled.

Principal Murphy picked up her big net. She ran out of the office. Miss Mopper left, too.

"I thought I was the only real monkey around here," I said to Claudia.

"Maybe you are." My sister led me into the hallway. "Maybe Miss Mopper was lying about seeing a monkey to get Principal Murphy out of the office."

"But why?" I asked.

Claudia quickly pulled me behind a large trash can. Then she pointed to something.

I peeked around the trash can.

I saw a tall ghost run past us and into the office. Then he ran out carrying Principal Murphy's new purse!

"It's the purse thief," I whispered.

"But why is he wearing a ghost costume?" Claudia asked.

"So if people see him running with the stolen purse," I said, "they won't know who he really is."

"They will think he is Roz," Claudia said. "Because of what happened yesterday."

"Unless someone catches the ghost," I said.

"You mean, someone like Principal Murphy?" Claudia asked.

"I mean, someone like the monkey me." I grinned.

Claudia looked worried. "If you change into the monkey, Clyde, you might not be able to change back."

"But I can't let the thief get away," I said.

I closed my eyes and thought about exciting things. Like visiting the science museum. Like turning into a monkey.

Like catching the ghost thief!

A wave of energy splashed through me. My head started spinning. My heart raced. Faster. And faster.

I sneezed.

TA-DAH!
IT'S MONKEY ME TIME!
CLYDE! STOP!
OOPS! YOU'RE RIGHT.
I FORGOT TO TAKE OFF MY HAT.
LOOK, CLAUDIA! MY BODY MATCHES MY MONKEY EARS.

CLYDE!
DON'T WORRY, CLAUDIA. THIS SHOULD BE EASY.
I JUST NEED TO FIND THE GHOST...
...BEFORE PRINCIPAL MURPHY FINDS ME.
UH-OH!

Catching the Ghost

NOW I NEED TO CATCH THE THIEF.
HA! NO ONE HAS SEEN ME STEAL THIS PURSE.
IF THEY DO, THEY'LL SEE MY GHOST COSTUME.
AND THEY'LL THINK I AM THAT KID, ROZ.
TIME TO USE MY MONKEY BRAIN.

HOW DO YOU STOP A GHOST?
YOU TAKE AWAY THEIR PURSE.
HOW DO YOU CATCH A GHOST?
YOU GET HELP.
TAP! TAP!

I HOPE THIS WORKS.
GIVE IT TO ME!

HA-HA!
NICE CATCH!
HA-HA!
NICER CATCH!
YOU'RE IN SUPER BIG TROUBLE THIS TIME, ROZ!

MISS MOPPER?!
CLYDE!
PRINCIPAL MURPHY CAUGHT THE PURSE THIEF, CLAUDIA.
AND IF YOU DON'T LEAVE NOW, SHE'LL CATCH YOU, TOO.

DID YOU SEE, CLAUDIA? I HELPED CATCH THE THIEF.
AND I SAVED ROZ FROM BEING PUNISHED.
WHAT I WANT TO SEE IS YOU CHANGING BACK INTO A BOY.
I'LL CHANGE BACK WHEN WE GET HOME.
I'M STILL TOO EXCITED...
...ABOUT BEING MONKEY ME, THE HERO!

I'M HOME.
SO NOW CHANGE INTO A BOY, CLYDE.
OH, NO! YOU CAN'T CHANGE BACK, CAN YOU?

YOU'LL BE A MONKEY FOREVER!
STOP WORRYING, CLAUDIA!
WHY?
BECAUSE YOU'RE MAKING ME WORRY, TOO.
AND WHEN I WORRY, I . . .

I'VE CHANGED BACK!
AND LOOK! NO MONKEY EARS!
BUT, CLYDE...
I'M HUMAN, CLAUDIA. SEE!
BUT, CLYDE...
I'M ME! CLYDE, THE BOY!
SO WHAT IS THERE TO WORRY ABOUT?

Timothy Roland is not a monkey. But he looks like one — when he wears his Halloween monkey mask. He also eats lots of bananas, juggles, and sometimes rides a unicycle.

Timothy lives and works in Pennsylvania. He has written and drawn pictures for over a dozen books, which he hopes will make children laugh (and make monkeys laugh, too).

Monkey Me
QUESTIONS & ACTIVITES
CAN YOU ANSWER THESE QUESTIONS ABOUT
MONKEY ME AND THE SCHOOL GHOST?
Why is it so important that Dr. Wally find a cure for Clyde?
Look at the picture on page 51. How does Clyde know that the thief is not Roz?
How would this story be different from the point of view of Principal Murphy?
Were you surprised that Clyde told the principal that Roz was not the thief? Why or why not?
Write a story about a real monkey getting loose in your school! Look up more about monkey behavior. What types of trouble could a real monkey cause?
scholastic.com/branches